George William Thomson

Verses from Japan

George William Thomson

Verses from Japan

ISBN/EAN: 9783337164416

Printed in Europe, USA, Canada, Australia, Japan

Cover: Foto ©Andreas Hilbeck / pixelio.de

More available books at **www.hansebooks.com**

VERSES FROM JAPAN.

LONDON: MDCCCLXXVIII.

NOTE.

Thefe little Poems were originally pub-
lifhed in the " Japan Weekly Mail."

G. W. T.

London, 1ſt January, 1878.

CONTENTS.

OMMÉ AND GENJIRO,

A LEAP YEAR LEGEND OF JAPAN.

IN the land of Yamaſhiro,
    In the ſweet and ſunny
        ſouth,
Singers love this touching ſtory,
    Paſſing it from mouth to mouth.

Youths and maidens lean to liſten,
    Paſſion's fiery thrill they know,
And in aged breaſts it wakens
    Tender thoughts of long ago.

Once upon a time a noble,
   Travelling from the city's din
With a crowd of carelefs fervants,
   Refted at a village inn.

Sojourn'd there a wicked warrior,
   Whofe fierce face with hot blood fhone :
Strange, each bore the name far famous,
   Oba Gendazaemon.

In the morning, when the funrife
   Bathed in light the land and fea,
Rofe the noble from his pillow—
   Rode unarm'd acrofs the lea.

And behind him his retainers
   Many a coftly burden bore,
When upon them furged that other,
   Like a wild wave on the fhore.

Filch'd had they his choiceſt armour ;
    Surely ſimpleſt child might con :
On the box-plate blazed in ſplendour,
    " Oba Gendazaemon."

Not one moment would he liſten ;
    Shook his frame with pent-up ire :
"Such miſtakes," he ſcreamed in fury,
    " I remit with ſword and fire."

Fierce and faſt like Noto's tempeſts
    Burſt his blows upon the train ;
Turn'd the noble at the clamour,
    Firſt he fell among the ſlain.

Dire as earthquake came the tidings
    To his waiting wife and ſon :
Dead! with Hope's gay buds ſtill breaking,
    Dead! with half his triumphs won.

Day and night on fleeteſt courſers,
  Like the winds that hilltops blow,
Through the ſtream, and o'er the moun-
      tain,
  Swiftly rode young Genjiro,

Till he came to where his father
  Lay in hovel dark and dead ;
Nervelefs lay the limbs of iron,
  Dreamlefs lay the kingly head.

Stung with fury vow'd the ſtripling
  O'er the land from ſouth to north,
He would track the baſe affaſſin
  And his daſtard ſoul drive forth.

And, that he might wander freely,
  Donn'd the boy a beggar's dreſs ;
But its coarſeneſs could not fully
  His ſurpaſſing comelineſs.

Tall he was, and ftraight as arrow,
　Fair his cheek, and forehead high;
Kiffo's eagles could not equal
　The proud glance that fill'd his eye.

From the firft faint ftreaks of dawning
　Scann'd he clofe the gaudy throng
That to Kanongfama's temple
　Swept in crowds the whole day long.

Here the merchant fleek and fmiling,
　There the noble proud and grave,
Here a group of laughing ladies,
　Like a foam-topp'd, funlit wave.

But the dark-brow'd, red-cheek'd vifage,
　With its black eye flafhing fire,
Never down the temple's alley
　Came to vengeance deep and dire.

One chill morn a maiden wealthy,
    Breathing prayer the temple fought;
From her *kango's* dainty cuſhions
    Peep'd her fweet face full of thought.

Clad in rags the fair boy beggar
    Braved the weather wild and wet;
Silver caſt the kindly maiden,
    And their eyes one moment met.

Rude difguife could never cover
    That lithe frame and beauteous face,
That brave eye and thoughtful forehead,
    That unconſcious, conquering grace.

Daily to the idol's temple
    Paſſes Yamaſhiro's Pearl,
And her parents fondly fancy
    Ommé grows a pious girl.

But when clouds of cherry bloffom
   Snow'd the ftony path to prayer,
Glanced fhe at the well-known corner;
   Ah! her darling was not there.

Never more to fee the glory
   Of his beauty, near or far;
She was like a fkiff on ocean,
   Searching for loft guiding ftar.

Sad fhe grew, the warm glow faded
   From her rofy, rounded cheek;
Head on hand fhe lay and languifh'd,
   Like a lily, white and weak.

Leaden-hearted lived her parents,
   While they watch'd her pale and pine:
Deep the heart of love-fick maiden,
   Deep as Sado's golden mine.

But one evening, when Death's fhadows
  Seem'd the fummer fields to fold,
To her mother faintly faltering
  She her long-kept fecret told.

Through her tears and fmiles fhe whif-
      per'd
  She could bear no other fate
Than to wed her heaven-fent idol,
  That bright beggar at the gate.

O'er the land they fought and found him :
  He had clofed his cruel queft,
For his fiery foe had fallen
  In the dark lands of the weft.

He had loved the winfome maiden
  From that firft fweet fmiling ftart :
Linger'd in his ear her accents,
  And her image in his heart.

All the joys that life can lavifh,
   When the foul is frefh and fair,
Through their foftly-gliding fummers
   Shed their fweetnefs on the pair.

Thus they tell the pleafant ftory,
   As the feafons come and go,
Of the love of gentle Ommé
   And the high-foul'd Genjiro.

From the cottage to the palace,
   From the cradle to the pall,
In all ages, in all countries,
   Love is ever lord of all.

LAMENT OF THE PRINCESS
OF MIKAWA

ON THE DEATH OF HER HUSBAND.

WANES the white moon, but not
the burſting heart
That brighter grows, and fuller
of its woe.
Time cannot leſſen ſorrow ſuch as mine.
The ſpring flowers bloſſom and the evening air
Is warm and fragrant, while with honied
throats
The orioles, from a maze of cherry
boughs,

Sing all the sweet love-secrets of their
    nests.
But oh! for autumn with her withering
    woods,
And skies that shed a thousand streaming
    tears!

The world's best jewel sank in death's
    dark stream,
And I, an empty bubble on the wave,
Live in the sunshine, while its light is
    gone.
They laid his body in the gloomy grave:
He went before me down the dreadful
    way
That all men travel, shuddering and alone.
Soon I shall follow, for the days fly fast:
Then, oh, my darling! through the mists
    of time

I fee our fouls together, foaring high,
Like eagles breafting the blue waves of
    heaven,
Rejoicing in the funfhine, far beyond
The whirring arrows of the hunter Death,
And all the many miferies of the world.

Now comes the quiet majefty of night,
With fleep's fair froft to hufh life's bab-
    bling ftreams.
Hufbands and wives lie down in blifsful
    reft :
Like golden lilies dreaming in the fun,
Fond women flumber in the arms of
    thofe
Whofe love lies round them, as the fap-
    phire fea
Circles the fragrance of an ifle of flowers.
Duft is your bed, beloved; mine is pain :

White are thefe cheeks where once the
　rofes blew,
Cold is this breaft that once was fill'd
　with fire,
For, till death comes, my own fweet love
　is dead.

LAMENT OF THE PRINCE OF CHOSHIU

ON THE DEATH OF HIS WIFE.

WAKING at midnight when the
world is ftill,
  Alone I feem to drift upon a
    tide
Of dreary waters, while the dying moon
Sinks flowly, gathering all her tender rays
And leaving the dark-vifaged night for-
    lorn.
Moans the wild wind : the air is fill'd
    with froft :
My eyes are dull, but folitude and cold,

Like cruel-throated watch-dogs, ſcare
    away
The timid traveller, Sleep.

                I cannot reſt :
A dear face ſhines upon me like a ſtar
Through death and darkneſs. Poor, ſweet,
    lonely love !
Oh ! I would be the ſtone upon her grave,
Or the leaſt flower that bloſſoms on her
    duſt,
But for the bleſſed hope that I ſhall meet
My darling ſomewhere in the ſilent land.
The rock of death divides the ruſhing
    wave,
But the twin ſtreams ſhall ſurely meet
    again.

Through the dim world the village temple
    bell

Touches my ears, and every ſolemn ſound
Repeats her name whoſe penſive thoughts
    were prayer.
My arms are empty, but my heart is full,
And ſhall be full of her for evermore.

FUMIFERA JAPONICA.

LIKE butterfly in sunbeam gay,
　　Or precious gem of dazzling ray,
　　Ohána is the brighteſt fay—
The ſweeteſt flower in Yedo;
Almoſt as fair ſhe is as thoſe,
With eyes of blue and cheeks of roſe,
Who dance till happy daylight goes
　　On daiſied Engliſh meadow.

Her eyes—dark wells of paſſion deep
Whene'er her ſoul is ſtirr'd—now ſleep
In ſunſhine, and her fancies leap
　　Like wavelets ſoft and ſtilly;
Her hair is bound with ſkill and grace;
Upon her laughing lips a trace

Of faffron flower is feen: her face
     Is powder'd like the lily.

As many-colour'd is her drefs
As that entrancing lovelinefs
Which fpans the rain-fwept fky to blefs
     The earth—a gladfome duty;
With *famifen* upon her knees,
And gaudy fan to coax the breeze,
She fits beneath embowering trees—
     A little Eaftern beauty.

But, fmiling, from her fleeve fhe takes
A tiny pipe, and gently breaks
The *kokubu's* beloved flakes,
     And lights a morfel gaily;
A whiff or two—the joy is done,
But fcarcely ere again begun.
She fmokes, I trow, if fhe fmokes one,
     Of pipes a hundred daily.

Alas! they caſt a ſhade on this—
The pureſt pearl of earthly bliſs—
The ſwift and ſweet delicious kiſs
　　Young lips ſoon learn the knack o':
I would not wed an angel bright,
With wings that fluttered ſoft and white,
And eyes that ſwam in liquid light,
　　If ſhe could ſmoke tobacco.

Then puff away all undiſmay'd,—
In curling clouds your graces fade;
No fervour ſhall your peace invade;
　　O exquiſite Ohana!
But on my knees I'd pray and pine,
In paſſion's agonies divine,
If only, ſweet, you would reſign
　　That vile Nicotiana.

THE LADY AND THE
FLOWER.

THERE was a **fweet flower**, red
and white,
That fill'd the gazer with de-
light.
Dropp'd in foft fhowers the fummer rain;
Joy bounded through each teeming vein.
Shone the glad fun, and round it roll'd
His quickening heat in waves of gold.
A lady from her chamber came,
And watch'd its bells in beauty flame.
Each jewell'd branch fhe clofely fcann'd:
Then, with the brighteft in her hand,

Acrofs the grafs fhe gaily fped,
And, fmiling, to herfelf fhe faid,
"Of flowers that bloom, or birds that
    fly,
Not one is half fo bright as I."
So, from the fun to grateful gloom,
She pafs'd into her fragrant room,
Took down the mirror from its place,
And gazed on her own lovely face.
Clofe to her cheek then held the flower,
Still fparkling with a filver fhower,
And foftly murmur'd, "Eyes that fhine
"Like cryftals—rofy lips are mine.
"The foolifh flower can never vie
"With this fair face—fo fweet and fhy."
Her hufband view'd the pretty fcene—
The bloffom in its robe of green—
The fmiling girl in filken drefs
Rejoicing in her lovelinefs,

And felt the thrill to monarchs known,
The darling vifion was his own.
Hearing his merry laugh fhe turn'd,
And afk'd with blufh that brightly burn'd,
"Which is more beautiful?" a fmile
Rippling around her lips the while.
A roguifh light was in his eye,
And jeftingly he made reply,
To draw into fome funny ftrife
His dear, vain, jealous little wife.
"The flower a thoufand times," he cried,
"Ah, would that it could be my bride,
"Fair as an angel from above;
"My foul is one wild fea of love!"
An angry flufh fwept o'er her brow:
"What think you of your beauty now?"
She faid: then dropp'd the bloffoms
  fweet,
And crufh'd them with her dainty feet.

THE WIFE'S APPEAL.

SINCE honeſt love lies dead
within your eyes,
And pity ſpeaks not in a ſingle
tone,
And no fond thought makes kind your
cruel touch,
Take a ſharp ſword and ſlay me. I muſt
die.
Ah! once my heart was like the rounded
moon,
Reflected in ſtill waters ; now it breaks,
Toſſ'd by the whirling eddies of deſpair.
Sweet were the days of youth, and ſweeter
yet

The golden fummers when your love was
      ftrong,

Before Omatfu bloffom'd into flower.

But when that brightnefs came, I faw
      your foul

Bend like a flender branch beneath the
      bird

That, flufh'd with fpring and weary of far
      flight,

Sinks, foft as fnowflake, on the rofy
      world.

Dreams the fair dove among the quiet
      trees,

Or fpeeds in funny fplendour o'er the
      fields :

What life more free and full of pleafant
      things ?

I am a foolifh bird whofe moffy neft

Is burn'd to afhes, and with wounded wing

I flit through flaming woods in pain and
fear.

Is there a ſhelter in the withering world ?

Where ſhall I go ? What friend can com-
fort me ?

O huſband, love or kill me where I lie.

THE WIFE'S TRIUMPH.

(THE HUSBAND SPEAKS.)

FIERCER within my breaſt the
    battle grew :
  Now ſweet Omatsu, gem of
    brighteſt ray,
Would lead me captive with a winning
  word ;
Then your fond looks would fill my heart
  with pain,
And your ſad face brings ſorrow to my
  dreams.
But, as the moon's reflection on the
  ſea

Still keeps its place though mounting
    billows roll,
Your fteadfaft purpofe lafted through the
    ftorm,
And I am drawn again to purer ways.
Stands a proud rock above a patient
    ftream
That wanders wimpling through pine-
    fcented glades
From fairy fountain on the purple hills.
No arrow fhot from ftrongeft archer's bow
Can pierce the cruel ftone. With angry
    frown
He fcorns the courting water of the
    ftream,
And cafts a carelefs glance upon her
    fmiles.
But undifmay'd the gentle current flows,
Lifting her loving arms in clofe embrace,

And making fummer fweeter with her
    fong :

Till, inch by inch, the hard rock melts
    away ;

The glad ftream rufhes through his
    inmoft heart,

And laughs and claps her tiny hands for
    joy.

Henceforward, Oh! my darling! there
    fhall be

Unclouded fkies and love that cannot
    change.

THE FADING FLOWER.

I WANDER'D where the sweet-
nefs of fummer made com-
pletenefs,
And all the woods were blufhing with
the fiery glow of flowers,
When fofteft winds were blowing, and
fongful ftreams were flowing,
And fped, alas! too fwiftly the honey-
laden hours.

I found amid the fplendour a little bud fo
tender,

I trembled with a thrill of joy I ne'er
 had known before ;
Like one in a fad ftory who turns a page
 of glory,
 Or fhipwreck'd failor nearing a fmooth
  palm-planted fhore.

With pride beyond all telling I bore it to
 my dwelling,
 And placed it where it fhone like ftar
  in night's engulfing gloom,
And there through years of gladnefs, or
 wearinefs and fadnefs,
 It fill'd with Heaven's own luftre the
  lonely little room.

Now, though its leaves grow crifper and
 cruel voices whifper,
 The flower has loft its beauty and
  groweth dim and old,

To me it beams as brightly as if it
quiver'd lightly
In morning's dewy frefhnefs, when
diftant hills are gold.

THE SWAN.

ALL in a foft and silent dream
 A bright bird, on a dimpling
  ftream,
 Floated through fheen and fhade:
The blue wave from her fnowy breaft
Fell fwiftly, though, with wings at reft,
 She fcarce an effort made.

To me fhe feem'd to glide along
As eafily as childhood's fong
 When fummer fkies are fair;
For who could fee the bufy feet
That 'neath the flowing waters beat
 With endlefs toil and care?

Somehow I mufed on lofty life
That fhow'd no trace of ftorm or ftrife,
   But fwept ferenely on,
Harmonious as the laws that guide
The throbbing ftar, the fwelling tide,
   While funlight round it fhone.

But none can tell the anxious thought
By which *that* ftately courfe was wrought
   Between its banks of flowers ;
The fleeplefs watch, the fecret pain
That almoft left the fpirit flain,
   The weary working hours.

THE ROSE AND THE RAIN.

 ROSEBUD in a garden gay
Hid all its fweetnefs from the
day :
Its crimfon leaves were folded faft,
Though funbeams foftly o'er it caft
Their golden glory, and the breeze
Sang of a thoufand fights that pleafe.
But rippling rain at length apart
Drew the green veftures from its heart,
And left it fmiling in the fun,
To life, and love, and beauty won.

Trembled the trees, the wind wax'd high,
Swept a fierce ftorm acrofs the fky,

The lightning like a sword-blade gleam'd,
From the black clouds a torrent stream'd,
And soon the radiant leaves empearl'd
Were scatter'd o'er the weeping world.

True love is like a silver shower,
That fills with light the summer hour;
But passion like a tempest sweeps
All loveliness to darksome deeps.
Bright heart of boyhood, ponder long
The meaning of the simple song!

THE BUTTERFLY.

KNOW a fair lady whofe face
    is a treafure
      That dazzles the eyes of all
    men with its ray,
But dreaming of naught but the paffing
    day's pleafure,
    She lives like a butterfly golden and
    gay.

In fummer's full glory, when fouth winds
    are fighing,
    And earth's floweft pulfes with fweet
    paffion ftart,
Amid the vaft joy, in foft ecftafies dying,

It choofes a bloffom and clings to its
heart.

But when tempefts gather and dim the
blue morning,
And mift-cover'd mountains frown
over the plain,
It leaves the poor plant its bright hues
were adorning,
And fpeeds with fwift wing from the
wrath of the rain.

Ah! light is the love that grows chill in
dark weather;
It fings in the funfhine, but pines in
the fhade;
Unlefs we can wander with brave hearts
together,
Go, find a new lover, my beautiful
maid!

A FAN SONG.

LITTLE fan, does never anger
   Stir your heart when all things
     lie
Steep'd in deep delicious languor,
  'Neath the funny fummer fky?

Sleep the billows on the ocean;
  O'er the fields no breezes ftray:
You alone with bufy motion
  Toil through all the drowfy day.

SONG.

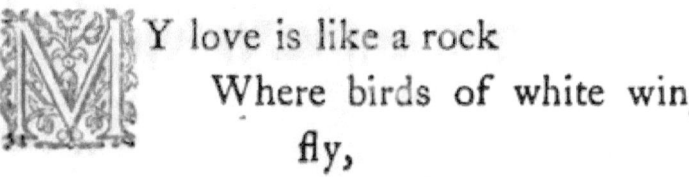Y love is like a rock
    Where birds of white wing
       fly,
Which billows overleap,
   And fun can never dry.

My fondeft fancies fpring
   Around him every hour,
Bound breaking at his feet,
   And o'er his brightnefs tower.

The gazer on the land
   Looks long acrofs the wave ;

He fees a ridge of fnow
　Where waters roll and rave.

The rock—it lieth low
　Beneath the tumbling fea ;
My darling's fteadfaft foul
　Is known to none but me.

SONG.

THE woods are green in summer-
      time
  And bright with bloſſoms gay :
The murmur of the happy leaves
  Sounds all the golden day.

But here a tree, by lightning ſtruck,
  Is black, and bent, and bare.
It lifts its arms like phantom fell,
  And dims the ſunny air.

A bird that built its dainty neſt
  'Mong branches bloſſom'd o'er,

Still fings upon the wither'd bough
  As blithely as before.

O fond and faithful as the bird
  That haunts the leaflefs tree,
Though darkeft clouds of forrow came,
  My fweet love ftay'd with me!

A THOUGHT FOR A FAMOUS FRIEND,

ABOUT TO TRAVEL NORTH IN WINTER.

CLOUDS in forrow come to-
gether;
    Wild and wet the winter
weather;
Dark night fhrouds the day with woe:
Cold and bleak the winds are blowing
Flocks of birds wing-weary going
South to where the funbeams glow.
When the blinding fnow falls thickly,
And your foul grows faint and fickly,

While your flow limbs ache and ſmart—
Though the ſport of chill December,
Over all the land, remember,
You lie warm in every heart.

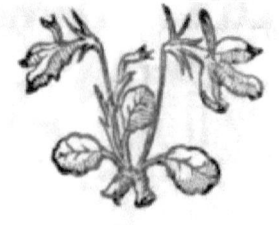

THE BEST PHYSICIAN.

WHEN I am fick,
　　O fend for him
　　Who fooner cures
Than doctors grim !

His prefence bright,
　His laughing eye,
Would make the god
　Of illnefs fly.

I hear his ftep ;
　He is fo dear,

All pain forgot,
  My brain grows clear.

Glad thoughts ſpring up
  Too ſweet to tell ;
He takes my hand,
  And—I am well.

SONG.

WHEN faſt I flew to my ſweet
    love,
    A thouſand miles ſeem'd one,
Though ſtormy ſkies made night above,
    Within me ſhone the ſun.

What matter if the way were wild,
    And white the cold ſea's creſt,
If I might reach, where ſummer ſmiled,
    The haven of her breaſt.

But now that far from her I go,
    Light of my lonely dreams;
Since every ſtep is ſad and ſlow,
    One mile a thouſand ſeems!

THE DREAM.

WAITED for my darling all
through the fummer noon ;
The crimfon flame of funfet
came, and then the filver moon ;
And hearing not in filence deep a bird or
bloffom ftir,
I laid me down and flumber'd, that I might
dream of her.

In fweet and fimple beauty, with blufh the
breezes gave,
As lithe as willow bending befide the
wimpling wave,

She rifes 'mid fleep's darknefs, like ftar
 through mift that fhines,
Or fairy flower in branching bower among
 the foreft pines.

The Spring is laughing from her lip, the
 Summer warms her breaft,
Upon her head the darkling fkies of cloudy
 Autumn reft,
While Winter takes her tiny hand and
 covers it with fnow:
Yet warm and foft its tender touch! My
 happy pulfes glow!

Alas! the joy is fading, the lovely face
 grows dim,
The vifion bright, the rofy light, in min
 gling fhadows fwim.

But o'er me bend delicious ſmiles, and
    eyes with love that beam :
Her own bright ſelf has broken her image
    in the dream !

THE LAST WORDS OF

MISAWA MENJIRO.

B E brave and faithful in your way:
Whatever foolifh men may fay,
Heaven fends to every earneft
soul
A light to lead it to its goal.
As beyond fight or fcent of fhore,
Bewilder'd by the breakers hoar,
The failor never wants a guide
Upon the ocean wild and wide;
By day the cranes in fteady flight,
By night the North ftar's lovely light.

C-1